Littlenose

More adventures of

Littlenose

Littlenose the Hero
Littlenose the Hunter

Littlenose the Joker

JOHN GRANT

ILLUSTRATIONS by ROSS COLLINS

SIMON AND SCHUSTER

SIMON AND SCHUSTER
Two-Eyes' Friends was first published in 1969
Squeaky was first published in 1977
Littlenose's Cousins was first published in 1979
The other stories were first published in 1983
in Great Britain by The British Broadcasting Corporation

This collection published by Simon & Schuster UK Ltd, 2007
A CBS COMPANY

1 3 5 7 9 10 8 6 4 2

Simon & Schuster UK Ltd
Africa House
64-78 Kingsway
London WC2B 6AH

A CIP catalogue record for this book is available from the British Library

ISBN 1-416-92667-4
EAN 9781416926672

Typeset by Ana Molina
Printed and bound in Great Britain by Cox & Wyman Ltd, Reading, Berkshire

Contents

Littlenose the Joker

Littlenose was a boy in a Neanderthal tribe, and Neanderthal folk were quite a merry lot. Despite the cold of the Ice Age, the frequent lack of food and the danger from wild animals, they enjoyed a joke as much as anyone. They could be heard laughing and singing as they worked at chipping flints to make tools, or cut and sewed animal skins to make clothes. And one of the most fun-loving Neanderthal people was Littlenose.

While Littlenose and his family and friends were ready for a laugh at any time, there was one day in the year which they kept especially for playing tricks on each other. They called it Crocus Day. As soon as the first crocus appeared in bloom in the spring, then for that day anyone could play tricks on anyone else, the person playing the trick shouting, "CROCUS!" at the person tricked. As you might expect, it was one of Littlenose's favourite times of the year.

One spring day, Littlenose sat under his special tree where he did his more important thinking. Two-Eyes, his pet mammoth was with him, half asleep in the first warm weather since the previous autumn.

"I don't know what I'm going to do, Two-Eyes," said Littlenose. "Any day now the first crocus will be out, and I haven't thought of a single trick to play."

"If you ask me," thought Two-Eyes in his own mammoth way, "the whole idea is a piece of nonsense!" But, as usual, nobody asked him, and Littlenose went on: "I could tie a rope across the cave entrance to trip up Dad . . . but I did that last year! Or I could tie a long string to the tiger-skin rug, and pull it so that Mum would think it was alive . . . but I did that the year before!" He thought a while longer, then, as it was almost lunchtime, he went home.

After lunch, he still hadn't thought of a good Crocus joke, so he decided to look over his collection, in case an idea might just come to him.

Littlenose was a very enthusiastic collector. His collection contained dried leaves, stones with interesting marks on them, birds' feathers, snail shells, and a piece of broken antler. By evening he still hadn't had any ideas, but the collection in his corner of the cave was looking much tidier. He had almost forgotten Crocus Day, and he said to Two-Eyes, "Let's go collecting tomorrow. I've a feeling I'll be extra lucky, and find something special to collect."

Next morning after breakfast, he slung his hunting bag across his shoulder and set off with Two-Eyes. They went along by the river, up the hill and into the forest, and in no time at all Littlenose had collected quite a few interesting items: a bird's egg, a large dead beetle, and a piece of bark with markings that looked vaguely like a picture of Dad. So much for the forest, now for the open grassland. He'd found some of the best items in his collection there.

But not this time, it seemed. "Keep looking, Two-Eyes," said Littlenose. Two-Eyes gave a sort of mammoth "Hmph!" and turned his head this way and that as he wandered in a casual sort of fashion through the long grass and around the clumps of gorse which grew here and there.

Suddenly, he stopped. "What is it, Two-

Eyes?" said Littlenose. "Have you found something?"

Two-Eyes made not a sound, but stood stock still, his big ears spread to catch the faintest sound, and his trunk held out sniffing delicately at the breeze. Some way in front was a particularly large clump of gorse, and as Littlenose followed Two-Eyes' gaze, he thought he could just make out something. Something big was lurking in the bushes. And things which lurked in bushes were invariably dangerous. He couldn't actually see anything among the foliage, but he could see what had attracted Two-Eyes' attention. A large object was sticking out from among the leaves. It was a horn. Not an ordinary horn, but one which was quite extraordinary. It was *huge*. It was half as big as Littlenose.

"That can only be one thing, Two-Eyes,"
he said in a whisper. "A giant wild bull!"

But Two-Eyes was a mammoth, and
mammoths had much keener eyesight than
Neanderthal boys. He also remembered
what Littlenose had forgotten. The great
wild bulls lived deep in the forest, and it
would be most unlikely to find one out on
the open grassland. Also, giant bulls didn't
usually stay as still as this, particularly if
people were near. He decided to have a

closer look. "No, don't, Two-Eyes," said Littlenose, as the little mammoth walked boldly up to the bush, reached up with his trunk, and touched the horn. The horn dropped to the ground with a soft thump. One thing was certain. There was no wild giant bull on the other end!

Littlenose ran to join Two-Eyes. He examined the horn. It was old and discoloured. And the sharp tip had been broken off. But it seemed worth collecting. It might be useful for keeping things in. Littlenose lifted up the horn and looked inside. It was full of dirt and dust, and he tried to blow it out, but his hair and eyes got full of dust as it blew back in his face. So, he turned it round, put the broken tip to his mouth, and blew again. There was another great cloud of dust . . . then a loud bellowing sound!

Littlenose
dropped the
horn as if it
were red-hot
and jumped
back, falling over

a tuft of grass and sitting
down with a thump. Two-Eyes was
nowhere to be seen. Littlenose cautiously
reached out to the horn and picked it up.
Two-Eyes equally cautiously peered out
from a distant clump of bushes. He walked
slowly towards Littlenose and looked
suspiciously at the horn. Timidly, he
touched it with the tip of his trunk.
Littlenose took a deep breath, and blew
hard into the horn. The noise echoed
across the landscape and set a flock of

crows cawing in alarm at the edge of the forest. This time Two-Eyes ran only a short distance before he stopped and came back sheepishly towards Littlenose. And Littlenose now knew why Two-Eyes had been frightened. The sound from the horn was exactly like the bellow of an enraged woolly rhinoceros. He gave it a more gentle blow, and it sounded like a slightly annoyed woolly rhinoceros.

This was a treasure indeed! Littlenose said as much to Two-Eyes. Two-Eyes grunted in a resigned sort of fashion. He knew what was coming next. He was right. Littlenose heaved the horn across Two-Eyes' back where it balanced precariously, and they set off back home.

They were not far from the caves when they saw two figures ahead of them. It was

Nosey and one of the other men returning empty-handed from a day's hunting. Littlenose liked Nosey, and he was about to shout and run after the men when he had a brilliant idea. Did the horn *really* make a sound like an enraged woolly rhinoceros? Maybe he and Two-Eyes had imagined it. They found a patch of long grass and hid. Then Littlenose lifted the horn . . . and BLEW!

It was wonderful! The two men dropped their spears and ran. "It's a woolly rhinoceros!" they heard Nosey yell. "ENRAGED! Run for your life."

Littlenose lay in the grass, and laughed and laughed until he was sore. Two-Eyes gave a sort of non-committal mammoth grunt. Actually, mammoths didn't have much of a sense of humour, and he thought the whole thing a bit ridiculous. When Littlenose had wiped the tears from his eyes, and peered over the top of the grass, Nosey and his friend had gone. "This is going to be fun," he said to Two-Eyes.

"This is going to lead to trouble," thought Two-Eyes. "As usual!"

The horn was much too big to join the rest of Littlenose's collection in his corner of the cave, so he hid it in a thicket near the edge of the woods. He would do something wonderful with it, but until he had decided what, it would be safe.

That day, Uncle Redhead was passing through the district, and dropped in for a visit. At supper, he said, "Spring's coming on fast. Any time now it'll be Crocus Day."

Crocus Day! Littlenose had completely forgotten. He had been so excited at finding the wonderful horn. And he still hadn't the faintest idea what tricks he would play. Uncle Redhead was in a reminiscent mood, and started to tell tales of Crocus Day tricks he had played when *he* was Littlenose's age. He had been the best joker in the district, throwing chestnuts into the fire so that they popped and sparked, startling everyone, or spreading bear grease on the stone floor at the entrance to the cave to make people slip and fall.

"Hmph!" said Mum. "It wasn't all *that* funny! I was the one who slipped!" She was, of course, Uncle Redhead's sister. But Littlenose thought it sounded hilarious. The snag was that it wasn't likely to come as a surprise to anyone after Uncle Redhead had been talking about it. He was really no nearer to thinking of a trick to play.

That is, until breakfast time the following morning. Neanderthal caves had no proper furniture, but handy rocks served just as well. Instead of a table, Littlenose ate his meals off a large flat rock, and smaller, round boulders, acted as seats. Littlenose was hungry, as usual, and he fidgeted as he waited impatiently for Mum to serve the food. As he fidgeted he was sure he felt his seat move. He wriggled, and sure enough the boulder rocked very slightly on the sandy floor of the cave. He was just going to tell Mum, when he had an idea. This might be the beginnings of a good joke. A Crocus Day trick that would be remembered for years . . . like Uncle Redhead's slippery floor. It would need a lot of preparation, and he couldn't start until he was sure of the right day.

Late that afternoon, Littlenose was playing in the woods with Two-Eyes when he saw something which made his heart leap. Among the long grass growing in a small clearing, he saw the dark spikes of crocus leaves. And among the crocus leaves were stalks with buds. And some of the buds were showing tips of colour. By tomorrow they would be crocus flowers in full bloom. Tomorrow would be Crocus Day.

Littlenose waited impatiently for the day to pass. Supper came and went. Then bedtime. Littlenose lay under the fur bed covers in his own special corner of the cave and worried. He was worried that the weather might suddenly turn cold or dull and the crocuses wouldn't open. And he was worried in case he fell asleep. The whole thing depended on staying awake until Mum and Dad were asleep. He had work to do. Hard work that had to be completed before getting up time.

At long last, apart from the occasional snore, silence fell on the caves of the Neanderthal folk. Littlenose slipped out of bed and tiptoed across the cave. The fire cast a warm glow of light, and a faint moonlight shone through the entrance.

Littlenose collected a handful of kindling and a flat piece of bone which he had hidden, and set to work. The sky outside was beginning to lighten with the coming day when he finished. He took a last look at his handiwork and went back to bed.

He had hardly closed his eyes, it seemed, when Mum was calling him. It was time to get up and fetch the water and the firewood. Rubbing his eyes, Littlenose got on with his morning chores, and it wasn't until he got back to the cave that he realised that Dad wasn't there. "Where's Dad?" he asked.

"Have you forgotten?" said Mum. "Dad has gone fishing with some friends. He left early. He won't be back until after breakfast. Breakfast isn't quite ready, so take your bedding out and give it a good shaking."

Bewildered, Littlenose dragged his fur

bedclothes out into the fresh air. His plan was going all wrong. It *depended* on Dad being at home for breakfast. He started shaking the dust and fluff out of the bedding. Suddenly, he gave a yell. "I've got something in my eye!"

"Let me look," said Mum. "Stay still! I can't see if you're jiggling about like that. Sit down." Still rubbing his eye, Littlenose followed her into the cave. "Here, where there's light to see," said Mum, and she pushed him down on the rock where Dad normally sat to eat. "Now, let's see . . ." Mum started to say. "Good gracious!"

Littlenose was lying flat on his back, and the rock seat had sunk out of sight into the sandy floor of the cave. Into the hole that had taken Littlenose half the night to dig! The pieces of stick holding the rock in

position had broken under his weight. But
it should have been *Dad* who collapsed,
when he sat down to breakfast. Then
Littlenose would have jumped up and
down shouting, "CROCUS!"

Mum said, "You're not hurt, are you?
Dad had better have a look at it when he
comes home. Let's see that eye of yours,
then we'll have breakfast."

Littlenose could have wept. What a start
to Crocus Day! He was sitting with Two-Eyes
under his favourite tree when he heard a
shout. People were hurrying from their
caves towards the river. From what they

said, Littlenose gathered that Dad and his friends had had extraordinary luck with their fishing, and the whole tribe was required to help carry home the catch. He might as well go along, too. Everyone was milling about among the high rocks along the river bank, their excited voices echoing loudly. Littlenose watched for a moment. Then a broad grin broke out on his face. He would play the biggest Crocus Day joke of all time. Involving the WHOLE TRIBE!

He raced to where the wild bull horn was hidden, and dragged it back towards the river and a handy patch of tall rushes. Then, puffing his cheeks out, he blew until he thought he would burst.

The bellowing sound blared out, echoing and re-echoing among the rocks. The people stopped in their tracks.

"A woolly rhinoceros!" cried one.

"ENRAGED!" cried another. And they ran and scrambled in all directions, falling over one another as the sound seemed to echo from everywhere at once.

"IT'S COMING OUT OF THE FOREST!"

"Across the river!"

"OVER THE HILL!"

And Littlenose lay among the rushes and laughed and laughed. He'd give them just one more for luck. Again the wild bellowing filled the air.

"It's getting closer," shouted someone. "Back to the caves!" Next moment it was a stampede.

"This is where I shout, 'CROCUS!'" thought Littlenose.

But as he opened his mouth, he realised

what had happened. The patch of rushes where he was hiding was between the river bank and the caves. Shouting in terror, the whole tribe raced for home, trampling through the rushes and everything else in their path, including Littlenose, who found himself flat on the ground under several dozen pairs of hard Neanderthal feet.

As the sound of the retreat faded in the

distance, Littlenose picked himself up, spitting out mud and pieces of rush.

"CROCUS . . . everybody!" he said, as he felt his bruises.

Two-Eyes appeared, wearing a very I-told-you-so look. Littlenose looked around for the horn. It was in a million pieces. "Come to think of it, Two-Eyes," he said as they set off home, "Crocus Day *is* a pretty silly idea anyway."

His immediate problem was to think of a good story for Dad regarding the mysterious behaviour of his rock seat.

And, in any case, it was another whole year before he would have to think of a Crocus Day joke.

Squeaky

Littlenose was one of the very few of the Neanderthal folk who kept a pet. He had Two-Eyes, the baby mammoth, and was very fond of him indeed. Yet, as Two-Eyes had found out very early on, being Littlenose's pet was hard work. Littlenose loved to play games with Two-Eyes, but he also loved to play tricks on him, and not very pleasant ones at that. The latest had

been when Dad had gone to look for gulls'
eggs in the marshes. Littlenose and Two-Eyes
went with him to help. However, as their
idea of helping was to run in all directions
at once, falling over tussocks, each other
and Dad, they were soon told to go away
and sit quietly.

Two-Eyes promptly lay down and fell
asleep, but Littlenose was bored. He started
to make a flower chain with marsh
marigolds, but it broke, and he threw it
down in disgust. Then he tried skimming
stones on a pool, until one of them just
missed Dad, who shook his fist at Littlenose.
Then Littlenose had a wonderful idea, and
he laughed just thinking about it.

He began picking the soft, fluffy heads
off the cotton grass. Then he tiptoed back
to Two-Eyes, who was still asleep, and

began to stick them on to the little
mammoth's black fur. Two-Eyes didn't
wake, and Littlenose gathered more and
more of the white tufts and stuck them on
until not a hair of black fur could be seen.
Two-Eyes was completely white. The real
fun came, of course, when Two-Eyes woke.

Mammoths were very fussy creatures,
forever preening their fur with their trunks,
and Two-Eyes went quite mad when he

found himself covered in cotton grass. He trumpeted and squealed, and he ran around pulling the white fluff off with his trunk. Then he saw Littlenose standing laughing. This was too much. He put down his head and butted Littlenose, who sat down with a thump, but didn't stop laughing until Two-Eyes had disappeared in the direction of home.

When he got home later with Dad, Littlenose was not really surprised to find that Two-Eyes was nowhere to be found. When Littlenose and his tricks became too much for him, Two-Eyes would sometimes go off to visit some wild mammoth friends for a week or two.

But, as the weeks became a month, then two months, Littlenose missed Two-Eyes very much. He became quite downhearted, and even the arrival of Uncle Redhead on a short visit didn't cheer him up much. In fact, he felt even *worse* because Uncle Redhead seemed to talk about nothing but pets. "There was this friend of mine," he said. "He had a pet lion. Bought it from a man for twenty red pebbles."

"Was it tame?" asked Mum.

"That's what my friend asked," said Uncle Redhead. "And the man he bought if from said, 'Sure, it'll eat off your hand'."

"Did it?" asked Littlenose.

"No," said Uncle Redhead, "it ate off his leg!" And he went into gales of laughter at his own joke.

Uncle Redhead left next morning. He shook Littlenose by the hand and said, "Goodbye and good luck," and gave him an apple. He didn't feel like an apple just then, so he put it carefully among his things in his own special corner of the cave.

When he did decide to eat his apple he had a surprise. There were small teeth marks on it. "Who's been eating my apple?" he thought. He wasn't long in finding out. He heard a scuffle and a squeak, and lifting up his fur hunting robe he saw a very small mouse crouched in a corner. It squeaked again and watched Littlenose with black, beady eyes. Littlenose stared back. It was a handsome little animal, with a glossy coat and a long tail. And it didn't seem all that afraid, for it stood up on its hind legs suddenly and squeaked even louder than before.

"I think it wants the apple," said Littlenose under his breath. And he bit off a small piece and carefully held it out. Just as carefully the mouse edged forward and took a gentle nibble before darting back to its corner. Littlenose laid the piece of apple beside it. "Here you are, Squeaky," he said. "You can be my new pet."

Littlenose played happily with Squeaky, who was very tame, until he heard Mum calling him for supper. Picking Squeaky up carefully, he took his place while Mum served the meal. Dad hadn't come in yet, and Mum was just filling a clay bowl with stewed rhinoceros, when she gave a terrible scream and leapt up on the large boulder, which served as a table. Littlenose jumped up in alarm, while Mum shrieked, "Get it out! Get that horrible brute out of here!"

Her cries brought Dad at a run. "What is it?" he shouted. "A bear? Sabre-toothed tiger?"

"A MOUSE!" cried Mum. "There!" And she pointed to where Littlenose stood, still holding Squeaky.

"It's Squeaky," said Littlenose, "look!" And he held Squeaky out for Mum to have a better look. But Mum didn't want a better look. She lifted the bowl of stewed rhinoceros above her head and cried, "Come one step closer . . ." She didn't need to say any more. Dad grabbed Littlenose by the scruff of the neck and ran him out of the cave. "Don't come back until you've got rid of it," he said, and trying to keep his face straight he went back in to comfort Mum.

"What on earth am I to do?" thought Littlenose. "I can't just leave Squeaky outside by himself. He might get eaten or stood on." Then he remembered his secret pocket. Neanderthal boys didn't as a rule have pockets, but Uncle Redhead had once shown Littlenose how to fashion one in his furs. Now Littlenose carefully tucked Squeaky into his pocket, where he curled up happily and promptly fell asleep.

Dad looked up as Littlenose came back to the cave. "Have you taken care of the mouse?" he asked.

"Yes," said Littlenose, quite truthfully, then sat down and got on with his supper. For a time there was silence except for the crunchings, slurpings and gurglings normal to a Neanderthal meal. Then Mum said sharply, "Stop fidgeting, Littlenose, for goodness' sake." Littlenose gave a sickly smile and sat still for a moment, but he was finding it more and more difficult.

Squeaky, after a short but refreshing nap in Littlenose's pocket, had decided to explore. Making his way through a mouse-sized hole in the pocket he was wriggling his way inside Littlenose's furs. His tiny claws scratched, and his tail and whiskers tickled, making it agony for Littlenose to sit still.

"What's the matter now?" said Mum, as Littlenose stopped eating and sat with hunched shoulders and screwed-up eyes. Before he could answer, Mum leapt up, scattering food in all directions and shouting, "There it is again!"

Squeaky had at length worked his way

right up inside Littlenose's furs, popped out at his neck, then leapt down to his supper. Littlenose didn't wait to be told this time. He grabbed Squeaky and fled, while Mum had hysterics and Dad shouted after him.

Littlenose made his way to his favourite tree, and sat down with Squeaky on his knee. "Much as I like you, Squeaky," he said, "as a pet you're not much of a success. Two-Eyes at least got me out of trouble from time to time, but all you seem to be able to do is get me into it." Squeaky said nothing, but Littlenose thought that he looked a bit sorry for all the upset he had caused. One thing was certain, squeaky could not return to the cave. Littlenose would have to find somewhere safe for him. He found an old,

cracked clay pot, into which he put
Squeaky with some berries for his supper.
Then he tucked it into a space among the
roots of the tree for safety. He said goodnight,
then went home to bed, hoping things
might have calmed down a bit by then.

By next morning, Littlenose had made
up his mind. He retrieved Squeaky from
the old pot and spoke to him very seriously.
"We are going to find Two-Eyes," he said.
"It's high time he came home. For one
thing, he knows how to behave as a pet
should, and can give you a few tips. For
another, you'll like him, although he is just
a bit bigger." Then he put Squeaky carefully
into his pocket.

Littlenose had thought that finding
Two-Eyes would be easy. He climbed a
high hill and gazed across the land hoping

to spot a lively mammoth herd, but nothing was moving as far as the eye could see. Then he tried looking for tracks. One thing about mammoth herds was that they left roads rather than tracks. As they moved from place to place they crushed the grass, flattened the bushes and trampled even small trees with their great feet. Even a single mammoth made footprints like no other animal. Yet Littlenose hunted high and low all morning without seeing as much as a crushed leaf or a single footprint. At midday he had decided to give up and go home, and was already on his way when he stopped and looked at the ground. The earth was sandy, and pressed into it was an unmistakable footprint. A mammoth footprint!

"It's Two-Eyes'. I know it is," he shouted

out loud. And he took
Squeaky out of his
pocket to have a look.
"Maybe he's already
on his way home,"
he went on,
completely
ignoring the fact
that Two-Eyes was a
baby mammoth and made fairly small
footprints. This was huge!

But minor details like that rarely bothered
Littlenose. He scouted around for more
footprints and quickly found another. Then
another. He could now make out a whole
line stretching into the distance. All he had
to do was follow them, and there at the end
of the trail would be Two-Eyes!

And a very long trail it turned out to be.

He even lost it at one point where it left the soft ground and crossed bare rock. He picked it up again at the edge of the forest, where it was so clear that he raced along with his eyes on the ground, not looking where he was going. Where he was going was right into a clump of bushes that had been chosen by a black bear for a quiet nap. It was just dozing off when the sky fell on its head. At least, that's what it thought.

Littlenose had blundered right over the bear and sat down hard on its head. The bear quickly leapt up, but Littlenose was quicker and was soon high in the branches of a tree, while Squeaky clung to a twig beside him. The bear stood on its hind legs, its head swaying from side to side as it tried to discover what had disturbed it. After muttering and grumbling to itself, it ambled away into the forest.

Waiting until the sounds of the bear had died in the distance, Littlenose scrambled to the ground. Then, with Squeaky safely back in his pocket, he hurried along the mammoth trail. It left the forest and began to cross the bare heath. Littlenose was by now very weary. The footprints led to a brownish-coloured hummock by a pile of boulders, and Littlenose made up his mind that he would sit down and rest there.

But halfway, he stopped in amazement. The hummock was growing. Higher and higher it rose, and he saw that what he thought had been brown grass or bracken was fur! The hummock was now standing on four mighty legs. Could it be . . .?

A glimpse of long curved tusks and a trunk told him that it could. It was a mammoth he had been trailing all right, but a very large grown-up one, not with a herd. Then he remembered his father speaking about rogue mammoths. They lived alone, and were more bad-tempered than anything you could imagine. The creature was half-turned away from Littlenose, and he hoped that it might go on its way without seeing him. Then it wheeled round, spread its ears and gave an almighty roar as it raised its trunk

in the air. Littlenose didn't wait to see what it would do next. He ran.

Almost immediately he felt the ground shake beneath him. The rogue mammoth was in hot pursuit. Its long legs ate up the distance between them. Its eyes were red and angry, and firmly fixed on the fleeing figure of Littlenose, while the sharp points of its tusks pointed straight at him. Littlenose glanced over his shoulder, and in that instant he tripped and fell. The roaring of the mammoth grew deafening.

And then there was a moment of awful silence.

Littlenose saw that the mammoth was no longer looking at him. It was gazing at something in the grass. Then it took a step backwards. It was shaking with fright, and instead of roaring, it squealed and whimpered, then turned in its tracks and ran. In no time at all it was out of sight. But what terrible thing had frightened a rogue mammoth? "Squeaky!" cried Littlenose. "I didn't know that mammoths were afraid of mice. I thought it was only

Mum." And he sat Squeaky on his shoulder and set off in the direction of home.

And who should be waiting for him when he got there but Two-Eyes. Littlenose threw his arms around the little mammoth. "How I've missed you, Two-Eyes!" he cried. "But you must meet your new friend, Squeaky." But Squeaky was nowhere to be found. Life as Littlenose's pet had proved just a bit wearing, and he had gone on his way.

Littlenose's cousins

Littlenose heard Dad shouting long before he reached the cave. There was nothing new in Dad's shouting, but this sounded different. "Probably something I've done," thought Littlenose, and he crept towards the cave entrance, trying to catch what Dad was shouting about.

"But it's only a one-apartment cave," Dad shouted again. "How can it possibly hold eight people? Why did you invite them in the first place?"

"We owe them a visit," came Mum's voice. "They were very hospitable when we visited them in the mountains. It's the least we can do."

Now Littlenose understood. His Uncle Juniper and his whole family were coming to stay. Uncle Juniper lived many days' journey away in the high mountains, where he gathered the berries of the juniper bushes for a living. Juniper berries were highly prized by the Neanderthal folk for making medicine, and every autumn Uncle Juniper came down from the mountains to sell his fruit at the market. He was really very famous, but because he lived so far away, very few people had actually met him.

Mum spoke again. "Nosey's wife told me

that her husband had met Juniper at the market, and that he had his whole family with him. So I sent a message asking them to stay for a few days."

Littlenose recalled his holiday in the mountains. Uncle Juniper had three boys who were, of course, Littlenose's cousins. But then, the Juniper family lived in a spacious two-apartment cave with plenty of room for visitors. Litttlenose began to understand why Dad had been shouting. The Junipers lived by themselves, with no neighbours nearer than the other side of the mountains. They were simple people, and Dad unkindly called them Country Bumpkins, Hillbillies and Yokels. Still, it would mean someone new to play with, and Littlenose began to look forward to his cousins' arrival.

The Juniper family arrived late on the afternoon a few days later. Littlenose shook hands with his Uncle, kissed his Aunt and turned to greet the boys.

"Hi, there, Littlenose," said the biggest cousin, giving Littlenose a rather too hearty thump on the back. "How does a mammoth get down from an oak tree?"

"Eh?" said Littlenose, still trying to get his breath.

"Sits on a leaf and waits for autumn," said the cousin. And the three of them shrieked with laughter, nudging each other and Littlenose and generally falling about.

"I suppose that's meant to be funny," thought Littlenose.

It was the same during the evening meal. The grown-ups were so busy talking among themselves that they paid no attention to the boys, and Littlenose found it difficult to get on with the important business of eating. First one, then another of the Juniper boys nudged him and whispered things like: "Why do mammoths never forget? Because no one ever tells them anything!" and, "What do you call a deaf mammoth? Anything you like; it can't hear you!"

Littlenose tried to edge away out of earshot, then Mum looked up and said, "For goodness sake, sit still and don't fidget. Look at your cousins! They're behaving themselves!"

At last it was bedtime, and Littlenose hoped that a good night's sleep might help things. But not a bit of it. The cousins giggled and whispered in the dark more of their stupid mammoth jokes, and when Littlenose said, "Please be quiet and let me get some sleep," Dad shouted, "Be quiet, Littlenose; you'll wake your cousins." It was all very unfair!

At breakfast, Littlenose decided that the best thing was to ignore the Juniper boys, even when they leaned right over and whispered in his ear, "How do mammoths catch squirrels?" He just looked straight in front and waited for Mum to serve breakfast.

"Don't be so rude to your guests, Littlenose," said Dad. "Answer them when they speak to you."

Littlenose sighed at the great injustice of

it all, but decided to say nothing, and had just started to eat when the smallest cousin said, "Look, Littlenose! Over there."

Heeding Dad's words, Littlenose looked, but could see nothing remarkable.

"Oh, it's gone," said the cousin, and Littlenose went back to his breakfast. It seemed to have an odd flavour, but he was hungry and tucked in just the same. The cousins were eating more slowly, and seemed more interested in watching him than in eating. The taste grew stronger the farther he got down his clay bowl. And when he reached the dead frog at the bottom he knew why. He also knew who had put it there. But before he could do anything about it, Mum chased the boys outside to play while she cleared up.

Two-Eyes, who had been made to sleep outside to make room for the visitors, came running up to Littlenose. Jumping on the little mammoth's back, Littlenose said, "Come on, Two-Eyes, let's go somewhere for a quiet think." And leaving his Juniper cousins to their own devices, they galloped away into the woods.

The first quiet thought that Littlenose had was to run away from home, at least until the visitors had gone. But his second thought was that it would be much easier to keep out of their way as much as possible. Having made up his mind, he went back to the caves. A lady called from one of them, "Hello, Littlenose. How are you today?"

"Fine, thank you," said Littlenose.

He was about to strike up a conversation when the lady stooped down and said, "I wonder who could have left this?" A large skin-wrapped parcel was lying by the cave entrance. She was just about to pick it up when the parcel gave a leap and bounced along the ground to disappear into a clump of bushes. At the last moment Littlenose saw the string and heard an unmistakable giggle. The lady had sat down with a thump and was shrieking her head off. People came running from the other caves. "It's that terrible boy," she cried, pointing at Littlenose. "Playing tricks like that! It shouldn't be allowed! It isn't good for people, that sort of thing!"

Littlenose tried to explain, but no one would listen. The cousins, meanwhile,

stood at the back of the crowd, grinning all over their faces.

Littlenose arrived home to a stern talk from Dad on the subject of annoying the neighbours. It was made even worse by Dad's insisting on referring to the cousins as perfect examples of Neanderthal boyhood. The evening meal was a repeat of the previous one, except that the supply of

mammoth jokes had apparently run out
and the cousins kept up a running stream of
equally unfunny jokes about sabre-tooth tigers.

At last it was bedtime. With eight people
it was a bit of a squash in the cave, but
Littlenose had managed to keep his fur bed
covers just a bit separate from the others.
With a sigh of relief at the end of a pretty
miserable day, he slid down beneath the
covers. Next moment he was leaping
around holding his foot and yelling at the
top of his voice. "Something bit me!"

Everyone came running, Dad pulled back
the bedclothes . . . and the
angry-looking hedgehog
which had been
trying to find a
way out since
the cousins had put

it in earlier, scuttled into a corner and rolled into a ball. Dad was furious. "You know the rules about pets," he shouted. "You're lucky I let Two-Eyes into the cave. Now, get that creature out at once." But the creature, guessing that it was not exactly welcome, and needing some fresh air anyway, had unrolled and vanished into the night.

Littlenose lay awake that night wishing he had decided to leave home after all. After breakfast next morning he went off and sat under his favourite tree, where he did most of his important thinking. He was quite alone, having managed to give the cousins the slip, while Two-Eyes had gone off on some business of his own. Littlenose considered all sorts of attractive schemes for getting his own back.

For instance, he knew of a cave in the forest which was the home of a particularly evil-tempered black bear. Supposing he could trick his cousins into thinking that there was some special treat in the cave! There would be for the bear! Perhaps he might lure them on to a floating log in the river and send them sailing all the way to the sea? Oh, dear, why did all the best ideas have to be the most difficult to put into practice? His daydreams were shattered by a sudden noise. Sudden noises usually spelled danger in those days, and Littlenose was about to take to his heels when he recognised something in the noise. It was a squeal, like that given by a small and frightened mammoth. Littlenose jumped to his feet. The squealing was coming closer, but it was accompanied by a strange jangling and clattering. The bushes parted, and Two-Eyes burst through, his eyes wide with terror. He was desperately trying to get away from a clattering collection of broken pots and old bones which came bouncing out of the bushes behind him, attached by a long string to his tail. There was no need to ask who had put them there. Two-Eyes ran to Littlenose, and in a moment the string was untied and the little mammoth sank breathless to the grass.

This was going too far! Playing tricks on Littlenose and even Neanderthal ladies was one thing, but to frighten a poor harmless creature like Two-Eyes was too much. Littlenose, of course, conveniently forgot that he spent more time playing tricks on Two-Eyes than anything else. He would have his revenge if it was the last thing he did.

And strangely, that very afternoon he got the inklings of a plan.

When Littlenose and Two-Eyes returned to the cave they found that the Juniper boys were still out, but that the grown-ups were sitting around the fire talking. Dad was saying, "Yes, the Old Man, the leader of our tribe, is anxious to meet you. He's asked me to invite you on his behalf to a reception tomorrow. I'll warn you now, he fancies himself at making speeches and you're likely to be bored to tears. But he usually lays on a good spread at these sorts of things."

"What about the boys?" asked Uncle Juniper.

"Oh, they can come in time for the food," said Dad. "We'll leave Littlenose with them. He knows where the place is."

Littlenose sat in his own special corner of the cave and hugged himself with delight. If he could work things right, he would have a magnificent revenge for himself, Two-Eyes and the neighbour lady. That evening, he sat with his cousins outside the cave chatting about this and that, and listening to more terrible jokes. During a lull in the conversation, he looked up and said with a sigh, "Well, I'm certainly glad it isn't me."

"What do you mean?" asked the oldest cousin.

"Surely they've told you," said Littlenose. "You've been chosen to be presented to the Old Man."

"What of it?" said the cousin.

"Ah, now I understand," said Littlenose. "They probably didn't want to worry you. I don't blame them. People have been known to run away from home to avoid being presented. I was scared stiff, I don't mind telling you, when it was my turn. That was when the Old Man gave me my special spear." Littlenose neglected to say that the presentation of the spear had been the result of a considerable misunderstanding, but that's another story.

The cousins were leaning forward now, eager to hear more. And Littlenose didn't disappoint them. "Listen carefully," he said. "This is very important." And Littlenose told them such a convincing story that by the time he had finished even he was almost believing it.

"The Old Man," he said, "is leader of the tribe, and to be presented to him is a great honour. But it isn't easy. Leaders of tribes aren't like ordinary men. That's why they're leaders. They are proud and fierce, with strange powers. Why, it's said that the Old Man can stop a charging rhinoceros with one glance. It's his eyes, you see, which are to be feared. No one has ever looked him straight in the eye and lived to tell of it! You will be presented to the Old Man tomorrow in the presence of the whole tribe; and because I have already done it, I have

been entrusted with seeing that you get
everything right. Because, if you don't . . ."
Littlenose paused dramatically, and the
cousins sat with mouths open in wonder.
"No wonder," thought Littlenose, "that
Dad calls them 'simple country folk'."

Before setting out for the Old Man's
reception the next day, Dad took Littlenose
to one side. "You'd only be bored with the
grown-up chat," he said. "Bring the boys
when the shadow reaches the pebble." And
he stuck a twig in the ground so that it cast
a long shadow in the sunlight, and placed
a pebble a little way ahead of the shadow.

As soon as the grown-ups had gone,
Littlenose turned to his cousins and said,
"Right. Time to get ready! Remember what
I said about the mud. It's to show that you
are truly humble in the presence of the

Old Man. And don't forget how you
approach him. On no account must you
look directly at his face." The three cousins
disappeared outside, and Littlenose quickly
moved the pebble a little farther from the
twig's shadow. The cousins returned and
started smearing handfuls of mud on
themselves. A ring round each eye. Patches
on each cheek. A dab on the nose. And
rings and dots on arms, legs and bodies.
Littlenose could hardly believe that they
were actually doing it. The shadow had
reached the spot which Dad had marked
with the pebble. "I must go on ahead,
now," said Littlenose. "Follow me when the
shadow reaches the pebble."

The grown-ups were gathered in the
sunshine outside the Old Man's cave when
Littlenose came wandering up looking very

downcast. "Where are the boys?" asked Uncle Juniper.

"Oh, they're messing about with mud and stuff," said Littlenose.

At that moment, a gasp went up from the assembled guests as three strange figures appeared. They were crawling on their hands and knees . . . backwards. Slowly they approached the Old Man, who said, "Well, bless my soul! What funny people." Someone tittered. "Stand up and let me see you," said the Old Man. They stood up, but with eyes shut tight, and the laughter grew at the weird spectacle of three boys covered in splodges of mud, eyes shut, and trembling with terror. Uncle Juniper wasn't laughing, however. "One of your local customs?" said the Old Man, turning to him.

Instead of replying, Uncle Juniper
grabbed at the boys, and cuffed their ears,
while they yelled, "But we thought . . ."
And the whole tribe laughed and laughed,
but no one laughed louder than Littlenose

- unless it was the lady neighbour.

That was the end of the visit. With the boys gone, Littlenose relaxed again, and was soon happily playing tricks on Two-Eyes as was, after all, only proper.

The Fox Fur Robe

It was a crisp Ice Age autumn day. The
Neanderthal folk were busy with preparations
for another Ice Age winter, collecting
firewood, gathering wild fruit and nuts,
and looking over their winter furs. The
men of the tribe were mainly occupied
with checking their winter hunting
equipment. They made sure that every
fire-making flint sparked properly . . . and

they spread out their hunting robes in the sun to air.

Littlenose spread his out on a flat rock close to the cave, and stood back to admire it. It was one of his proudest possessions, and he explained to Two Eyes: "Mum made my hunting robe for me. She hadn't enough of any one fur, so it's really a bit of everything. Bear, squirrel, rabbit, wolf. And fox . . . with a tail. It's the only hunting robe in the tribe with a tail. Probably the only one in the whole world." Two-Eyes tried to look interested. He had his own fur coat and didn't need a robe, and he hid a mammoth yawn behind his trunk as Littlenose chattered on.

Dad came out of the cave with his hunting robe over one arm. He shook out the dust and carefully put it on, the hood

over his head. Mum came out of the cave
after him.

"You're not wearing that terrible old
thing, are you?" she asked.

"What's wrong with it?" said Dad.

"It's ragged, and torn, and worn. And it's
full of holes," said Mum.

"But, apart from that?" said Dad.

"It's a perfect disgrace," said Mum, going

back into the cave. "To the family . . . and to the whole tribe!"

"What do you mean, 'disgrace'?" shouted Dad after her. "I'm the best hunter."

"And the worst dressed!" echoed Mum's voice from inside, followed by a loud rattling of cooking pots bringing the conversation to an end.

Dad went off by himself, muttering, "Disgrace, indeed!" And Littlenose turned back to his own hunting robe, which was in very good condition.

Over the evening meal, Dad sat, brooding. He wouldn't admit it, but Mum was right. There was a market in a week's time, the last before the Ice Age winter closed in and made travelling even more difficult than normal. He might just pick up an end-of-season bargain. He cleared his throat.

"Thinking of going to the market," he said casually. "Anything you need?"

Mum smiled quietly to herself. "There's the odd thing I could do with. Bone needles. A new bone ladle."

"Right," said Dad. "I'll take Littlenose and Two-Eyes. It's time that Littlenose learned something about trading. He could do worse than watch me in action. When it comes to driving a hard bargain—"

"Yes, we know," said Mum. "And Two-Eyes can help carry all your hard bargains home."

When market day came, Dad hauled Littlenose out of bed while it was still dark. The sun was only just coming over the hills when they left the caves behind. Littlenose had visited the market several times, and the way never seemed to get any shorter. As usual it was noon before they reached the circle of trees on the hill where the Neanderthal folk gathered to trade and exchange furs, flints, spears, axes, food, drink, and gossip.

After a quick snack, Dad started a tour of the various traders, while Littlenose trailed behind him and Two-Eyes took himself off to a sheltered spot for a nap. They passed several men selling household articles like bone needles and ladles, but Dad's mind seemed to be on other things. At last, they stopped at the foot of a tall tree where an old man sat cross-legged beside a great heap of furs. "Now," said Dad to Littlenose, "watch closely. The first rule is never to appear too eager to buy! Haggle about the price. That's the secret to driving a hard bargain."

"Can I help you?" said the old man.

"Thank you," said Dad. "Just browsing." And he began to rummage among a heap of black bear-skin hunting robes.

The old man beckoned to Littlenose. "You seem a fine young fellow. A credit to your noble father, I'm sure." And he handed him an apple. Littlenose said, "Thank you," and took the apple. "Yes, I said to myself," said the old man to no one in particular, "a person of distinction. A chief at the very least. Am I right?"

". . . er, not exactly," said Dad.

"Not at all," thought Littlenose.

"A person of breeding. And taste. Very rare these days, and a joy to behold . . . and serve. Allow me, sir." The old man stood up and took Dad's arm, and guided him over to another pile of furs partly hidden by the tree. "A more exclusive selection," said the old man. "For those who really know about such things."

Littlenose watched in astonishment. Dad, his eyes alight, was holding the fur robes up one after the other. These were none of your common black bear or grey wolf. They were snowy white, gold and brown striped, yellow with brown spots. Dad was almost drooling with excitement as he hauled out from the foot of the pile a hunting robe, the likes of which Littlenose had never seen before. It was an exquisite creation in fully-fashioned red fox fur. Or, at least, that's how the old man described it, as he slipped it on to Dad's shoulders and stood back.

"How much?" said Dad, hoarsely.

The old man shook his head. "It's not for sale. It's made to measure for a high

chief of the Mountain People. To be
collected today. Sorry."

Dad just stood as the old man took the
red fox fur robe, folded it carefully and
placed it on top of the heap. Littlenose
thought this was strange - why wasn't
something to be collected today on top of
the pile already?

"Another time, perhaps," the old man

was saying as Dad walked away with a very strange look.

"What about the haggling and the hard bargain bit?" thought Littlenose.

For the rest of the afternoon Dad wandered about looking at the various things for sale. He bought a bundle of bone needles and a ladle, but nothing else from the list which Mum had given him, while Littlenose looked for something to buy with the five white pebbles he had earned doing odd jobs for the neighbours.

At length, as the sun slipped lower in the sky, they found themselves back by the tree where the old man sat with his furs. He called over to Dad. "This is indeed your lucky day, your lordship. I've just had some very sad news. The high chief of the Mountain People was eaten this afternoon.

By a sabre-tooth tiger."

"You mean . . .?" said Dad.

"Yes," said the old man. "The red fox fur robe will go to waste unless, that is, someone of good taste and—"

"I'll take it!" shouted Dad. "How much do you want?"

"Now," thought Littlenose, "is where we see some real hard bargaining." But, to his astonishment, when the old man said, "Twenty green pebbles," Dad didn't even pause as he went on " . . . and I'm giving it away. Taking the food out of the mouths of my wife and children . . ."

Dad was already pouring his coloured pebbles out of their leather pouch and desperately counting them. Red ones, green ones, a few yellow, and a handful of white. He muttered to himself, counting on his fingers, then he turned to Littlenose. "I'm five white pebbles short. Have you any?" Littlenose hesitated for a moment, then handed Dad his pebbles.

With shaking hands, Dad thrust two handfuls of pebbles at the old man and snatched up the red fox fur robe. "A pleasure to do business with you, sir," said the old man.

"I bet it is," thought Littlenose.

Two-Eyes was surprised not to be laden down with a pile of Dad's purchases. But Mum was even more surprised when they arrived home. It was dark, and Mum was busy at the back of the cave. She saw the figure in the red fox fur robe in the light from the fire and hurried forward. "I'm afraid my husband isn't home yet, sir—" she started to say, then stopped. "Good gracious! It's YOU!" she cried, and sat down with a thump.

Littlenose came into the cave. "It's Dad's new hunting robe," he said. "Fox fur. Fully-fashioned."

Mum was too astonished to say any more. Dad gave her the needles and bone ladle, then, being careful to avoid making creases, he sat down to wait for Mum to bring supper.

It was late, and they went to bed as soon as they had eaten, Dad very reluctantly taking off his new robe.

When Littlenose woke next morning, Dad had already gone out. He came in just as they were sitting down for breakfast . . .

and he was wearing the fox fur hunting robe. "Just been for a stroll," he said. "Air's marvellously fresh this time of the morning." He sat down, and Mum began ladling out his breakfast. A tiny drop splashed out of the clay bowl. Dad cringed back. "Careful!" he shouted. "Don't throw it about like that! It's everywhere!" And he rubbed and scrubbed at an invisible spot of breakfast on the red fur.

After breakfast, Littlenose prepared to go out to play with Two-Eyes. The weather had turned mild, and Mum said to Littlenose, "I don't think you need wear your winter furs." Dad had to go to see Nosey the tracker on a matter of business, and Mum watched in amazement as he settled the new robe neatly on his shoulders and smoothed the fur with his hands before going out into the warm sun.

Long before Dad reached Nosey's cave, Nosey saw a large crowd approaching. In front was Dad, pretending not to notice the other hunters who pointed at the red fox fur robe and shouted things like: "It's the new autumn fashion! Red fox? Red face, you mean!" And the man was right. Dad was boiling under his hunting robe, and his face glowed crimson. But he tried to ignore his discomfort, as he ignored the remarks.

"I'll take your robe," said Nosey, as Dad entered the cave.

"No, no. It's quite all right," said Dad hastily. "I'm not stopping more than a few moments."

"Please yourself," said Nosey, as Dad sat down and surreptitiously wiped his brow with the back of his hand. The business, about the last hunt before the winter, was settled quickly.

During the week before the hunt, Dad was hardly to be seen without his red fox fur hunting robe, and after a time people got used to it and stopped making humorous remarks.

On the day of the hunt the men of the tribe gathered at dawn in front of the caves. By this time the weather had turned definitely wintry, and they all wore their hunting robes. They were made from brown bear, grey wolf, and only one was red fox! If nothing else, Dad was conspicuous!

The hunting party set off, led as usual by Nosey and his incredibly sensitive nose. Through the forest they went in single file, the apprentice hunters (including

Littlenose) bringing up the rear. Then Nosey held up his hand and the hunters halted, while Nosey crouched low and sniffed and snuffled among the pine needles. He stood up, pointed, and whispered, "There, thirty . . . no, I tell a lie . . . twenty-nine paces away is a bull elk."

That was good news. There was enough meat on a bull elk to feed the tribe for several weeks. The hunting party began to circle around through the trees to get downwind of the elk, their hunting robes making them almost invisible as they merged with the shadows beneath the trees. Well, almost! Everybody merged . . . except Dad. The red fox fur of his hunting robe positively shone out, and Nosey signalled with his hand for Dad to get back behind a tree trunk. But it was too late.

The elk came grazing its way into the
clearing where the Neanderthal hunters
waited, hidden amidst the gloom of the
forest. Then it stopped. What was that?
Something man-sized and bright red. The
bull elk hadn't got where it was by hanging
around asking questions . . . even of itself!
It turned in a flash and crashed through

the undergrowth and was gone.

Nosey jumped up and down with vexation, and in true Neanderthal fashion they all stood and shouted at each other, particularly at Dad, before they moved on to try again. Again Nosey's wonderful nose led the way, while Nosey muttered about lost opportunities, and they'd be dashed lucky to get another chance. But they did, almost straight away.

The trees were thinning out, there was very little cover, when Nosey said in a loud whisper, "Down, everybody!"

A small herd of deer was feeding and hadn't spotted the hunters, who dropped flat in the grass. Except one. Dad looked at the ground. It was damp and a bit muddy. One couldn't go around throwing oneself down on any old patch of ground, particularly wearing fully-fashioned fox fur robes. He knelt and began carefully to brush away some loose twigs and dead leaves. He covered the muddy bit with a handful of grass, then began gingerly to lower himself on to his stomach, taking care not to wrinkle his hunting robe. The hunters watched in total disbelief. And so did the deer . . . for a split second. Then they were gone, in a flash of white tails and a rattling of antlers on low branches.

There was absolutely no doubt whose fault it was this time, and Dad was made to go to the rear of the column, behind even the apprentices, where, it was decided, he could do the least harm.

And off trudged the hunting party once more.

"That's two chances we've missed," said

one. "I don't really suppose we'll get another."

"No," said another man. "It's only accidents that come in threes. But that's really two we've had already. What's going to happen next?"

"Oh, something really terrible, like an earthquake," said his friend, and they went on, braced for the next disaster. It came a few moments later.

Dad's voice came urgently from the tail of the column. "Listen! What's that?"

Behind them they could hear a thudding, rumbling noise accompanied by a crashing of undergrowth and getting closer every moment.

"An earthquake! I knew it!" cried someone.

Then, with a snort and a bellow, the "earthquake" was upon them. Bursting out of the trees came the most ferocious animal of the Ice Age world. Even the sabre-tooth tigers were afraid of the forest cattle, and it was the biggest imaginable forest bull which thundered down upon the Neanderthal hunters, the sharp tips of its great horns shining dangerously in the sunlight.

Someone shouted, "RUN!" which was a bit pointless, since the hunters were already scattering in all directions before the bull had caught more than its first glimpse of them. Before it had reached the centre of the clearing they were already safely in the branches of tall trees!

Except one!

While his companions sprinted for safety, their hunting robes flying wildly about them, Dad shambled as quickly as he could, hampered by the elegantly close-

fitting lines of his fully-fashioned red fox fur hunting robe. The bull whirled round, looking for its vanished victims, and saw Dad desperately trying to hitch up the robe as he ran. At the last moment he managed to sidestep the charging animal, and before it could turn for another charge he untied the strings which fastened the robe and pulled it off. Then he ran like the wind for the trees, the red fox robe over his arm. But, fast as he ran, the bull galloped faster. When the hoof beats were right behind him, Dad again side-stepped, and the bull passed so close that the wind almost knocked him off his feet.

From the safety of the trees, Littlenose and the hunters watched in astonishment as Dad ducked and dodged the bull. Every time Dad got close to a tree, the bull was somehow there first, ready to charge again.

After a particularly wild charge by the bull, Dad stood panting in the centre of the clearing, the red robe in one hand and trailing on the ground, and the bull glared with fierce red eyes from the edge of the forest, pawing at the ground and tossing its horns. Dad looked round for the nearest tree, and he had his back to the bull when it charged. He whirled at the last second, the robe flying out, and the bull raced past, skidded to a halt and came at him again. This happened several times, then Littlenose suddenly shouted, "It's the ROBE! It's not YOU it's after, Dad. It thinks the ROBE'S ALIVE! Drop the robe and save yourself!"

"Not likely!" shouted back Dad as he leapt yet again to safety. "This robe cost me twenty green pebbles. No bull's going to get it . . . no matter how big it is!" And he pirouetted quite gracefully with the robe flying over the bull's horns which missed Dad by a hair's breadth.

The hunters clung to their branches, astounded. It was really very exciting. Littlenose didn't know that Dad could be so agile, but then it wasn't every day that Dad had a giant forest bull after him with its long sharp horns. But Dad was beginning to tire. As the bull charged he just stood and swung the robe in a circle so that the bull skidded by under his outstretched arm, and Nosey leaned from his tree and shouted, "Olé!"

Dad looked up at the sound of Nosey's voice, and in that moment the bull caught the tip of one horn in the hem of the robe,

nearly pulling
Dad off his
feet before
it was torn
from his
grasp.
While the
bull knelt
on the fallen
robe and ripped
and slashed at it with
its horns, two of the hunters dashed across
the clearing and dragged Dad to the safety
of the trees.

The last sight any of them had of the
red fox fur hunting robe was a glimpse of a
tattered fragment flying from the tip of a
horn as the bull, with a triumphant snort,
disappeared into the depths of the forest.

That is, if you don't count the squidgy patch of trodden earth, mashed-up grass, leaves and fragments of red fur in the middle of the clearing.

"That was my fully-fashioned red fox fur hunting robe," wailed Dad, almost in tears. "I'll never have one like that again."

"Good," said Nosey, unsympathetically.

As they prepared to set off home, Littlenose said to Nosey, "Mr Nosey, what was that you shouted back there? When Dad dodged the bull? 'Olé!' or something."

"I don't really know," said Nosey. "It just seemed sort of appropriate."

And he set about sorting out the party into their correct order for the trek back to the caves.

Two-Eyes' Friends

Littlenose's best friend was Two-Eyes, his pet mammoth. Great herds of wild mammoths roamed the land. They usually kept clear of the places where people lived, but occasionally, if food was scarce, they would be seen close at hand, and Littlenose had several times watched from a safe distance as a herd went by.

The young mammoths were the same

size as Two-Eyes but the grown-up ones towered as tall as trees, with long powerful trunks and enormous curved tusks.

One day, Littlenose was playing one of his own very complicated games outside the cave where he lived. It involved twigs and stones and patterns in the sand, and was so intricate that only he really understood it. Two-Eyes, who was supposed to be playing, eventually gave up and wandered away by himself.

He made his way up the hill behind the cave and on to the grassy upland beyond. It was a lovely day, and a fresh wind was blowing.

Two-Eyes snuffed at the breeze with his trunk. It was full of all sorts of interesting smells. He took another snuffle, and his eyes grew round with excitement. His ears spread out and his trunk held straight in front of him, he trotted forward, following an unusual scent. It grew stronger every moment, until he came to the edge of a hollow, and saw something that made him squeal with delight.

It was a huge herd of mammoths!

The great males were standing on the edge of the crowd, keeping watch for any cave lion or sabre-toothed tiger who might fancy a piece of mammoth steak for lunch. The females gathered in groups exchanging mammoth gossip, while there were dozens of young ones, like Two-Eyes, running and jumping and playing all over the place.

Two-Eyes gave a little squeal and trotted down into the hollow. The young mammoths stopped playing and watched him suspiciously. One of them came over to Two-Eyes. They snuffled at each other and grunted and squeaked in mammoth talk, and a moment later were firm friends. The others crowded round, and they too squeaked and grunted at Two-Eyes, and soon it was as if they had known each other all their lives.

Then the games started again. They ran races, played tug-of-war with their trunks, and did a wonderful dance. Each held the

tail of the one in front in his trunk, while
they wound their way in a long snaky line
through the hollow, much to the annoyance
of the grown-ups.

Two-Eyes was enjoying himself so much
that he forgot the time. Only when the sun
was getting low in the sky did he realize
that it was late, and that he ought to be
thinking of going home.

He trumpeted "Good-bye" to his friends
and started to leave. But they didn't want
him to go! They came running after him, and
crowded round, while Two-Eyes desperately
tried to explain that he had to go.

They would come too, they squealed;
and Two-Eyes couldn't make them
understand that he lived in a cave with
Littlenose and his mother and father. The
mammoths didn't want to be parted from
their new friend, and in the end, Two-Eyes
set off with them all crowding round him.

Meanwhile, Littlenose had realized that
Two-Eyes had not returned, and it was

getting near bedtime. He stood at the cave entrance and called: "TWO-EYES!"

But there was no answer.

He called again, and was just about to set off to look for him in the woods when, looking up, he saw a black shape appear on the crest of the hill behind the cave. "Come on, Two-Eyes," he shouted. "It's late. Almost bedtime."

The black shape started running down the hill, and Littlenose was about to turn away when he gasped in horror. Not one, but dozens of little black mammoths were coming over the crest. Like a black, furry wave they poured over and down, heading straight for the cave. Littlenose turned to run . . . but he was too late.

The mammoths swept past and over him, knocking him off his feet. In a cloud of dust, and squealing and snorting, they rushed straight into the cave.

Pots broke, the supper was trampled underfoot, the fire was stamped out and Mum and Dad were pushed up flat against the back of the cave.

Mum was speechless . . . but Dad wasn't!

"LITTLENOSE!" he screamed. "Get them out! This is all your fault! Get these stupid creatures out before they knock the whole place down!"

Littlenose got safely behind a tree this time before he called: "TWO-EYES!"

Two-Eyes heard and came running out of the cave . . . but so did all the others. Once more the black furry tide swept around Littlenose, but this time it didn't knock him down.

"Please, Two-Eyes," said Littlenose. "I

don't know which one is you. Couldn't you please ask your friends to go home, and only you come when I call?

But of course the friends didn't want to go. They stood, pressed close around Littlenose, waiting to see what would happen next. They were enjoying this new game.

In the cave, Dad and Mum looked at the damage. It was dreadful. There was hardly a thing that hadn't been broken.

"That mammoth is the stupidest creature I know," said Dad, angrily.

"I'm sure he didn't mean it," said Mum, soothingly. "He was only playing with his friends. He's brought them visiting, and they want to meet us."

"Well," said Dad, "they won't get a second chance," and he began to block up the entrance with rocks, leaving only a space at one side.

"Come on, Littlenose," he called. "Hurry, or you'll be locked out."

"But I can't come without Two-Eyes," Littlenose wailed. "He can't stay out all night, and I don't know which is Two-Eyes. They all answer when I call."

"Two-Eyes should have thought of that before he started all this foolishness," called back Dad. "Now hurry. It's getting dark."

Littlenose was desperate. He just couldn't leave Two-Eyes out all night, but how was he to tell which one was his pet?

Then he remembered. Of course! How silly could he get? Two-Eyes got his name

because his eyes were different colours – one red and one green. Other mammoths had two red eyes, all Littlenose had to do was look.

It took ages. The mammoths' long shaggy fur hung down over their eyes, and he had to go round each one, stroking it and carefully parting the fur over its eyes to see the colour. He had looked at more than half before he found Two-Eyes.

Dad was making impatient gestures from the cave, so Littlenose quickly leaned over and whispered in Two-Eyes' ear: "Do as I tell you, Two-Eyes, and go very slowly. We don't want this lot charging into the cave again. Now, come along."

Taking Two-Eyes' trunk in his hand, he led him slowly through the closely crowded mammoths. Those in front made way for

them, while those behind fell in to make a
sort of procession. Gradually, they drew
nearer to the cave. Littlenose let go of the
trunk, and began to steer Two-Eyes from
behind, aiming at the gap in the barricade.

Then, just as Two-Eyes's head was in the
cave, Littlenose gave him an enormous
push, while at the same time he whirled
round with a yell and waved his arms.

Two-Eyes scrambled into the cave, while the mammoths scattered in all directions. Littlenose jumped inside, and Dad quickly blocked the opening.

All night the little creatures cried and whimpered outside for their friend. Occasionally, a small trunk would poke through a chink in the rocks, and no one got a wink of sleep.

However, just before daybreak, they heard the most dreadful noise. There were loud trumpetings and crashings and the thunder of many great feet. Dad peeped out.

"It's the mammoths!" he cried. "They've come for their young."

The adults were very angry with the young ones for running away, and were slapping and spanking them with their trunks while chasing them home. The loud

noises went on for a long time, but
eventually died away in the distance.

In the morning, everything looked a bit
flattened, but otherwise there was no sign
of the mammoth herd.

Later in the day Littlenose climbed up
to the hollow. But the mammoths had gone
from there too, and although in the
following weeks Two-Eyes visited the
hollow hopefully, they never came back.

If you enjoyed reading *Littlenose the Joker*, here's an extract from the next book, *Littlenose the Explorer*

Littlenose's Hibernation

It had been snowing all night; come to think of it, it had been snowing all week. The Ice Age landscape was covered in snow . . . and ice, of course. In the caves of the Neanderthal folk, snores came from under fur bedclothes, while the sun rose reluctantly over the trees, its pale winter light shining into the caves to tell people that it was time to get up.

Littlenose poked his berry-sized nose out of the covers, and quickly pulled it back again. He screwed up his eyes and shivered.

"If I had my way," he thought, "no one would get up at this time of year. Everyone would stay in bed until spring." He pulled the covers closer around his ears, but only succeeded in letting in a cold draught.

The cold draught was nothing to the icy blast which hit him as Father dragged the covers off. "Up you get," he shouted. "You can't lie there all day. There's work to be done. We're out of firewood, and Mother needs water from the river before she can make breakfast."

Pulling on his winter furs, Littlenose left the cave and trudged through the snow towards the river, a clay pot on his shoulder and a stone axe in his hand. "Fill that pot! Chop that wood! That's all I ever hear these days," he muttered to himself.

He muttered while he broke a hole in the river ice with the axe and filled the pot with water. He was still muttering as he brought it back to the cave, and he continued to mutter as he chopped a branch from a dead tree and dragged it home. "Stop muttering," said Mother. "I think you must have got out of bed on the wrong side this morning."

"If I had my way," thought Littlenose to himself, "I wouldn't have got out of any side of the bed at all."

Over breakfast, he continued to think: "People are stupid. Birds and animals have more sense. The elk left months ago for warmer places to spend the winter; and the wild geese flew far away to the south where it is always summer."

The last course for breakfast was a few

hazel nuts. Littlenose crouched close to the fire to eat them. "Squirrels eat nuts," he said to himself. "They collect them in the autumn and only get up to eat one or two, if they wake up feeling peckish. They sleep more or less all winter. I wish I could do the same."

Suddenly, he jumped up, scattering nuts all over the floor. Why couldn't he sleep all winter, hibernate like the squirrels and the bears and the dormice? But it was not something to be done on the spur of the moment. It required a lot of thought.

That night after supper, Father sat with an air of great concentration, binding a new flint point on to his spear, and Mother was sewing. Littlenose hesitated for a moment, then spoke to Mother. "I'm going to hibernate," he said.

"Well, do it quietly, dear," said Mother, without looking up. "Don't disturb Father. You know what he's like when he's busy."

Littlenose started to say something, but decided not to. He had tried to tell them about his intentions and it shouldn't come as too much of a shock.

The shock was Littlenose's next morning. When Father as usual pulled the covers off him, Littlenose pulled them right back on again. "I'm hibernating," he said, eyes shut tight. Next moment, he was standing shivering outside the cave where Father had yanked him by one ear. His winter furs landed at his feet, and Father shouted, "Get dressed, and stop this nonsense! There's work to do."

As he did his morning water and firewood fetching, Littlenose muttered more than usual, but he had to admit to himself that he had handled the whole scheme very badly. The problem was that the cave wasn't his; it was Father's. And Father made the rules. Bears and other hibernators prepared special places to spend the winter. He would have to do the same.

As soon as Father and Mother were busy, Littlenose slipped into his own special corner of the cave and gathered up his bedding, plus a few fur rugs that no one appeared to be actually using at that precise moment. Then, looking like a large, round, furry animal with no head and two legs, he left the cave and set off through the snow. A cave of his own was what he was looking for. Not too big. Just somewhere he could roll up in his furs and dream the winter away. It was more difficult than he had imagined. Caves weren't that easily come by, and they all appeared to belong to someone already.

Littlenose was a long way from home when he spied the dark opening of a cave among a pile of boulders. About time, too, he thought. Although it was winter, the noonday sun was warm, particularly to someone laden down with fur bed-clothes. He looked carefully around; there were no signs of a fire or anything else that might suggest people. Cautiously, he entered. The cave seemed spacious and had a soft, sandy floor. Might as well give it a try. Littlenose spread out the furs, then lay down and rolled himself up in them. It was perfect. And it seemed such a pity after coming all this way to waste such a find.

He would start his hibernation there and then.

Littlenose woke with a start. Was it spring already? He didn't feel as if he had slept for very long. Something hit him gently on the head. He put his hand up to feel. His hair felt wet, and something hit the back of his hand . . . a drop of water.

Littlenose jumped up. He could hear it now. A steady drip, drip! He looked up. The sun must be melting the snow, and the cave had a leaking roof. No wonder nobody lived here. He gathered up his bedding before it got too wet, and hurried out into the open again.

Well, the day was young. Still plenty of time to find a suitable cave. And only a short distance away, partly screened by a clump of bare trees, was another opening in the side of a high bank.

This time, Littlenose was taking no chances. He left his fur covers outside and carefully examined the floor for puddles and damp patches, and peered as well as he was able, into the gloom above his head for any sign of a leak. It seemed perfect! The trees outside cut off most of the light from the very back of the cave, but Littlenose groped around and spread the fur rugs and bed covers into a comfortable bed. Then he rolled himself up and closed his eyes to await the coming of spring.

Littlenose woke slowly. He felt quite refreshed. Was it spring already? Well, there was one way to find out. He made to push back the bed-clothes . . . and had a horrible surprise. He couldn't move!

Something seemed to be holding his

arms tight. He couldn't move his body, although his legs seemed to be free. What had happened? Was it magic? Had he perhaps blundered into a Straightnose cave and they had put a spell on him? He tried again, and found that he could move one hand and arm just a bit. He began to investigate with his fingers. All he could feel was the fur of the bedclothes. He could recognise each piece by the feel. There was the grey wolf skin with its long, soft fur. And the short soft fur of the cover made from many rabbit skins stitched together. And the tiger skin rug. The red fox. The bear skin. The . . .! Wait a minute!

HE DIDN'T HAVE ANY BEAR SKIN COVERS!

100,000 YEARS AGO people wore no clothes. They lived in caves and hunted animals for food. They were called NEANDERTHAL.

50,000 YEARS AGO when Littlenose lived, clothes were made out of fur. But now there were other people. Littlenose called them Straightnoses. Their proper name is HOMO SAPIENS.

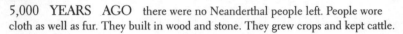

5,000 YEARS AGO there were no Neanderthal people left. People wore cloth as well as fur. They built in wood and stone. They grew crops and kept cattle.

1,000 YEARS AGO towns were built, and men began to travel far from home by land and sea to explore the world.

500 YEARS AGO towns became larger, as did the ships in which men travelled. The houses they built were very like those we see today.

100 YEARS AGO people used machines to do a lot of the harder work. They could now travel by steam train. Towns and cities became very big, with factories as well as houses.

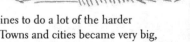

TODAY we don't hunt for our food, but buy it in shops. We travel by car and aeroplane. Littlenose would not understand any of this. Would YOU like to live as Littlenose did?

Littlenose

the Hunter

Littlenose is learning to hunt. He has to practise tracking dangerous animals and spear-throwing. Sometimes he's even allowed to join the grown-ups on hunting expeditions.

But being a caveboy is a dangerous business – there is plenty of opportunity to get into dangerous scrapes, and Littlenose is particularly good at that. He just can't stay out of trouble!

ISBN: 1-416-91090-5

the Hero

Littlenose doesn't go to school but he still has plenty to learn: how to track animals, how to find his way through the forest and which berries are good to eat and which are poisonous.

But whether he's exploring caves, taking a trip down the river or rescuing his father from a deep pit, somehow Littlenose always seems to end up in trouble!

ISBN: 1-416-91089-1